TORTUGA IN TROUBLE

by **ANN WHITFORD PAUL**

illustrated by

ETHAN LONG

Holiday House / New York

With love and appreciation to Paula, Ernesto, Sofia, and Erik.
A. W. P.

To my Mom and Dad, and to God, for this amazing and toilsome talent of mine.
Thank you, with love.   E. L.

Text copyright © 2009 by Ann Whitford Paul
Illustrations copyright © 2009 by Ethan Long
All Rights Reserved
Printed and Bound in China
The text typeface is Barcelona Book.
The illustrations were done in gouache and colored pencil.
www.holidayhouse.com
First Edition
1 3 5 7 9 10 8 6 4 2

Library of Congress Cataloging-in-Publication Data
Paul, Ann Whitford.
Tortuga in trouble / by Ann Whitford Paul ; illustrated by Ethan Long. — 1st ed.
p. cm.
Summary: When Tortuga arrives at Abuela's house to bring her supper,
Abuela looks suspiciously like Coyote. Includes a glossary of Spanish words used.
ISBN 978-0-8234-2180-0 (hardcover)
(1. Fairy tales. 2. Turtles—Fiction. 3. Desert animals—Fiction. 4. Grandmothers—Fiction.)
I. Long, Ethan, ill. II. Little Red Riding Hood. English. III. Title.
PZ8.P2818To 2009
(E)—dc22
2008006791

GLOSSARY OF SPANISH WORDS

abuela	ah-BUEH-lah	grandmother
adiós	ah-dee-OS	good-bye
amigos	ah-MEE-gos	friends
canasta	cah-NAHS-tah	basket
conejo	co-NAY-ho	rabbit
culebra	cu-LAY-brah	snake
dientes	dee-EHN-tess	teeth
ensalada	en-sah-LAH-dah	salad
flan	FLAHN	a sweetened egg custard
hola	OH-la	hello
ojos	OH-hos	eyes
orejas	or-EH-has	ears
tamales	tah-MAH-les	Mexican dish of minced meat sealed in cornmeal dough
tortuga	tor-TU-gah	tortoise

One day when the sun rose
Tortuga said,
"Iguana, please lift this
canasta onto my back."
"Conejo!" Iguana called.
"Culebra! I need help."

Conejo hopped. Culebra squirmed. And they lifted the basket onto Tortuga's shell.

"What's inside?" asked Iguana.

"Supper for Abuela," Tortuga said. "Grandmother loves *ensalada, tamales,* and *flan.*"

Conejo rubbed his belly. "Salad, tamales, and custard! Yum!"
"We should come with you," said Culebra.

"In case your *canasta* falls off," Iguana added quickly.

"You don't fool me, *amigos*," said Tortuga. "You may be my friends, but what you want now is this supper. I'll do fine by myself." And he started on his way. The three *amigos* watched Tortuga disappear down the road.

"*Adiós, ensalada* and *tamales*," said Conejo.
"Good-bye, *flan*," added Culebra.
"It doesn't have to be *adiós*!" said Iguana. "Let's follow Tortuga." And they did.

When the sun reached the top of the sky, Tortuga met Coyote.

The three *amigos* hid behind a cactus.
"Where are you off to?" asked Coyote.
"I'm taking supper to Abuela," said Tortuga.
Coyote peered into Tortuga's *canasta*.
He licked his chops.

"I just remembered!" Coyote said. "I'm late for an appointment." Off he raced. The three *amigos* rushed out.
"You shouldn't talk to Coyote," said Iguana.
"He wants to eat your supper," said Culebra.
"And you, too," added Conejo.
"Nonsense!" said Tortuga. "Coyote won't bother me. He has an appointment. Go away." Tortuga went on down the road.

"*Adiós, ensalada* and *tamales*," said Conejo.
"*Adiós, flan*," added Culebra.

"No *adiós*," said Iguana.
"Let's keep following him!"

And they did.

When the sun set, Tortuga finally reached the house of his *abuela*. "Supper's here!" he called. "Come in. Come in," answered a voice.

"That doesn't sound like his *abuela*," said Iguana.

The three *amigos* peered in a window.

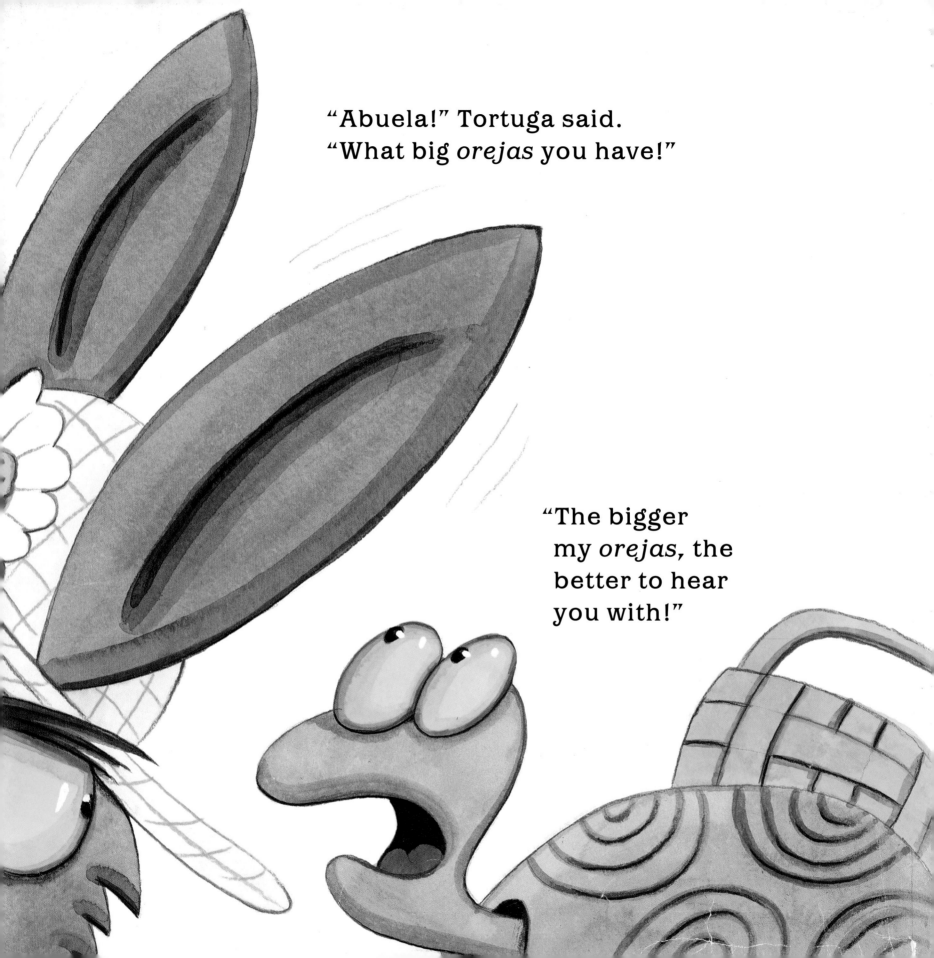

"Abuela!" Tortuga said.
"What big *orejas* you have!"

"The bigger
my *orejas*, the
better to hear
you with!"

"Abuela!" Tortuga said. "What big *ojos* you have!"

"The bigger my *ojos*, the better to see you with!"

"Abuela!" said Tortuga. "What big *dientes* you have!"

"The bigger my *dientes*,
the better to **EAT** you with!"

Coyote grabbed the *canasta* and shoved Tortuga into the closet with Abuela.

Then Coyote set a kettle of water on the stove. He put the *ensalada, tamales,* and *flan* on the table. Coyote drooled.

Conejo sighed. "This really is *adiós, ensalada* and *tamales*."
"*Adiós, flan*," said Culebra.
"And *adiós*, Tortuga."
Iguana flicked her tail angrily.
"We have to do something!"

She whispered to her *amigos,* "Here's my plan."

Then Iguana SLAP! SLAP! **SLAPPED** her tail against the house.

Culebra shook his rattle as hard as he could. RATTLE! RATTLE! RATTLE!

Conejo hopped BUMP! THUMP! against the house. BUMP! THUMP! BUMP! THUMP! BUMP! THUMP!

Coyote's *orejas* perked up. His *ojos* grew round.
And his *dientes* chattered.

"Help! Monsters!" Coyote raced out the door and across the desert.

Iguana, Culebra, and Conejo waved *adiós*. Then they hurried inside and opened the closet. "We heard monsters!" Tortuga said. "Did you see them?"

"It was us," said Iguana. Culebra said, "We made that noise."

"To scare Coyote away," added Conejo.

"What good *amigos*!" said Tortuga.
"Without you, Abuela and I would be soup.
How can we ever thank you?" Tortuga
looked at the table. He looked at his *amigos*.
"I know! Come share our supper."

"*Hola, ensalada* and *tamales!*" said Culebra.
"Hello, *flan,*" added Conejo.
"*Hola* is much better than *adiós,*" said Iguana.
"Dig in," said Tortuga.

And they all did.